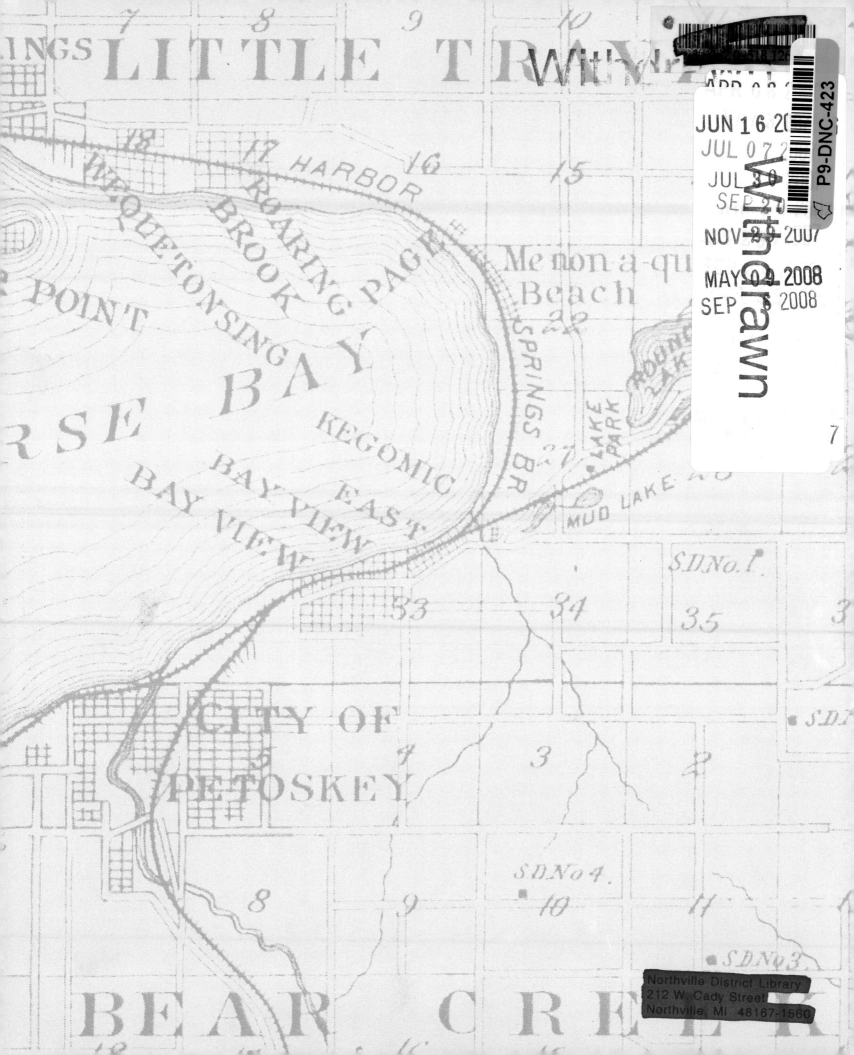

The Legend of the Petoskey Stone

By Kathy-jo Wargin
Illustrated by Gijsbert van Frankenhuyzen

I would like to extend my full appreciation and gratitude to the Little Traverse Historical Society for opening their doors and allowing me access to their collection. I would also like to give heartfelt thanks to their director, Candace Fitzsimons, for her personal help, insight, and knowledge. As well, to all my wonderful friends, many of whom shared their views of Petoskey history and Petoskey Stones with me. To my assistant, son Jake, who gave his input through many drafts, pushing me forward to make it better each time. And to Ed, thank you for showing me the promise of tomorrow.

—*Kathy-jo Wargin*

I always rely on the kindness and willingness of friends and family to pose as models for my books. "Petoskey" is no exception. Thanks to Kelly and Robbyn, for always helping me in a pinch. Thanks to neighbor and good friend Kelvin Potter, for posing as the "older" Chief and to his nephew Alex Potter, for becoming the "teenage" Chief Petoskey. Much gratitude goes to Kevin and Craig Wilkinson for the lengthy time they spent in my studio "playing their parts." Many thanks to Larry Charness. The first time I saw him I knew I would someday use him as a voyageur in a book. And finally, my appreciation goes to the all the parents who drive their kids back and forth to my studio. Your patience makes my job easier.

—*Gijsbert "Nick" van Frankenhuyzen*

Sleeping Bear Press
310 North Main Street, Suite 300
Chelsea, MI 48118
www.sleepingbearpress.com

© Thomson Gale, a part of the Thomson Corporation. Thomson and Star Logo are trademarks and Gale and Sleeping Bear Press are registered trademarks used herein under license.

Printed and bound in Canada.

10 9 8 7 6 5 4 3 2 1

Library of Congress Cataloging-in-Publication Data
Wargin, Kathy-Jo.
The legend of the Petoskey stone / written by Kathy-Jo Wargin ; illustrated by Gijsbert van Frankenhuyzen.
p. cm.
Summary: Recounts the life of Petosegay, an Ottawa Indian chief, who gave his name to the small town in northern Michigan— Petoskey—where a unique stone can be found along its shores.
ISBN 1-58536-217-4
1. Ottawa Indians—Folklore. 2. Stone—Michigan—Petoskey—Folklore. 3. Petoskey (Mich.)—Folklore. [1. Petosegay, Chief, 1787-1885—Legends. 2. Ottawa Indians— Legends. 3. Indians of North America—Michigan-Legends. 4. Folklore— Michigan—Petoskey. 5. Stones—Folklore.] I. Frankenhuyzen, Gijsbert van, ill. II. Title.
E99.O9W37 2004
F-dc22   2003026231

About the Legend of the Petoskey Stone

More than 350 million years ago, the five Great Lakes were one warm and shallow sea filled with large colonies of living coral. Over time, the earth went through many changes. Ice ages came and went, and as Pleistocene glaciers scoured the region, they plucked this petrified coral from the bedrock and scattered it primarily throughout northern Michigan in the form of fossilized coral we have come to know as *Hexagonaria percarinata*, or Petoskey Stones.

For more than one hundred years, Petoskey Stones have been beloved treasures from northern Michigan. In this story, we learn the connection between them and Ignatius Petoskey.

Ignatius Petoskey, as he became known later, was born *Be do se gay*, which through time became *Pe to se gay*, which was later anglicized into Petoskey. Because he was born in 1787, there is not an abundance of documentation or illustrations of his life along the shores of northern Michigan, however, the information that remains does help to create a picture of his successful life and how he was named beneath the "rays of the rising sun." In my version of this story, where legend and history meet, I hope you discover the beautiful richness of his life, and find special meaning in every Petoskey Stone.

—Kathy-jo Wargin

A father and his son were
walking along the beach, searching for
Petoskey Stones. They looked through
rocks that had washed up near the water's
edge, they sifted through sand and pulled
stones from the shallows of Lake Michigan.

The father was watching the water roll toward shore
when all of a sudden a wave splashed at his feet. It was
then he spotted the wet, gray stone. It was round and
smooth, and had a beautiful sunburst pattern upon it.

As he plucked it from the sand, he asked his son, "Has
anyone ever told you the story about the Petoskey Stone?"

Long ago in 1787, an Odawa Princess and her husband were leaving their winter home. He was a French fur trader who had been welcomed into her tribe as an honorary chief, and he had worked through the winter collecting furs in an area we now call Chicago.

But when spring arrived, it was time for them to travel back to their summer hunting grounds along the shores of northern Lake Michigan.

The family traveled day after day, but the journey was slow and hard because the Princess was ready to give birth. One night, as they neared the mouth of the Kalamazoo River, she could not travel any further. The family made a shelter, and while the Princess remained behind the deerskin door of the hut, her husband waited outside, listening to night sounds and admiring stars in the sky.

The Princess began to give birth to
the baby as the chief waited nearby.
Hours passed and the stars dimmed.
The moon began to fade and the night
animals became quiet. But then as it
became almost silent, only moments before
the sun was ready to rise, the joyous cry of a newborn
child filled the woods and echoed over the water.

The chief held the baby in his hands, feeling deep and instant love. At that moment the sun rose, casting ribbons of beautiful light through the trees. As sunshine fell softly upon the baby's face the father said,

"He shall be Petosegay, and he shall be an important man."

He named him Petosegay because the word meant the rays of the rising sun, or sunbeams of promise. He knew this was a good name because it meant there was always the promise of a new day.

As his father adored him, Petosegay was bathed in the most beautiful morning light, and it seemed as if the nearby lakes, rivers, and forests whispered his name in approval.

Not long after, the family
reached their village in the
north woods where the
baby known as Petosegay
grew into a
young boy.
He loved to
play in the lake, and
could easily catch the
biggest and best fish.

Petosegay also liked to hunt for food.
He would walk quietly through the woods,
and always, when he found his game,
he was thankful and useful with it.

And when the snow arrived, Petosegay went in search of animals for their fur. Furs would keep his family warm, or be traded for goods. He set traps and snares in the forest, and grew better at the challenge every year.

As Petosegay grew to manhood, he became such a skillful hunter that one year he killed 40 bears and sold their hides for a very good price.

Over time, Petosegay became a fur trader like his father had been. He traveled by water to Indian villages, collecting furs. He piled his birchbark canoe high with pelts and raised a sail made from an old blanket. As it gathered breeze and pushed him along, he sailed through an inland waterway to the east side of Michigan. From there, he pushed on to Mackinac Island where he would trade them for goods.

Petosegay loved his homeland along the shores of northern Michigan. It seemed as if all of nature belonged to him, and that he had a special place along the bay.

Eventually, Petosegay married and became a father. He was now a headman, which meant he was third in line in his tribe. This was a place of honor, one that he earned through his intelligence and fairness.

Over the years, Petosegay was such a successful trader, hunter, and farmer that he was able to purchase land near a beautiful river that danced like a ribbon through the forest and flowed right into the big lake. It was known as the place where bears walked beside the flowing waters, and Petosegay liked it very much.

So Petosegay built a wooden home there at the edge of the lake, settling on the shore where the sand rippled in waves among small gray stones.

But things were beginning to change.

A town was beginning to grow in the area near Petosegay's home. Pioneers came from the east to build homes deep in the woods. Farmers came to plow long stretches of grass into farms. Business people came to build lumber mills and stores.

One man, Hiram O. Rose, came to set up a general store and other businesses. He quickly became friends with Petosegay and began to call him Chief Petosegay as a sign of respect. Because most people knew Petosegay and liked him very much, it wasn't long before the whole town began to call him Chief as a sign of admiration.

But the growing area needed an official name, so one night several people gathered to choose just the right one. It didn't take long for everyone to agree that it should be named Petoskey, after Chief Petosegay. True to the words his father spoke the moment he was born, Chief Petosegay was becoming an important man by lending his name to the town he loved. And in return, Petosegay was loved by all.

It wasn't long before people from
other places wanted to visit the town named
after Petosegay. Some came by steamship, while
others came by train. They came to enjoy the beautiful
lake and to breathe the fresh air, but they also came to
walk along the shore and search for a special stone that
appeared to hold the rays of the rising sun inside. Because
the stones seemed to be found everywhere near Petoskey,
they soon earned the name Petoskey Stones.

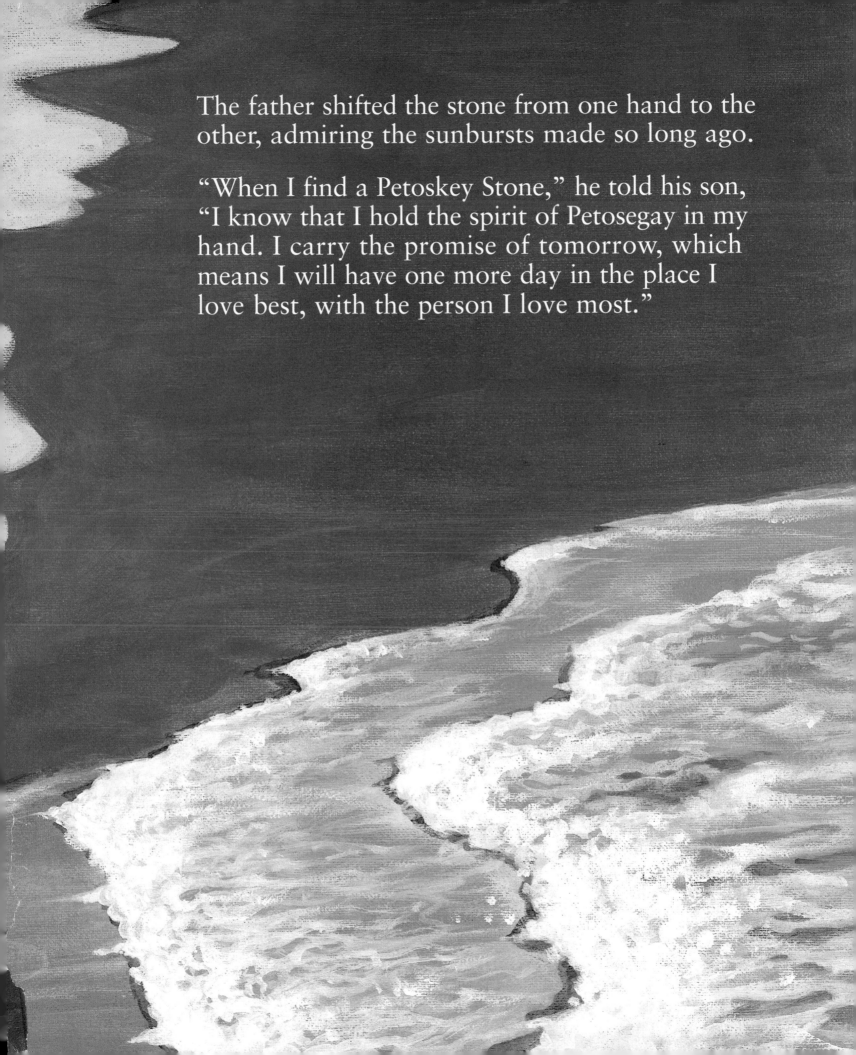

The father shifted the stone from one hand to the other, admiring the sunbursts made so long ago.

"When I find a Petoskey Stone," he told his son, "I know that I hold the spirit of Petosegay in my hand. I carry the promise of tomorrow, which means I will have one more day in the place I love best, with the person I love most."

With that, the father placed the Petoskey Stone into his son's hand and whispered, "That place is here, and that person is you."

The little boy held the stone as tight as he could and looked at his father with love. And just then, as sunlight fell upon them, it seemed as if all the nearby lakes, rivers, and forests whispered Petosegay's name once again.

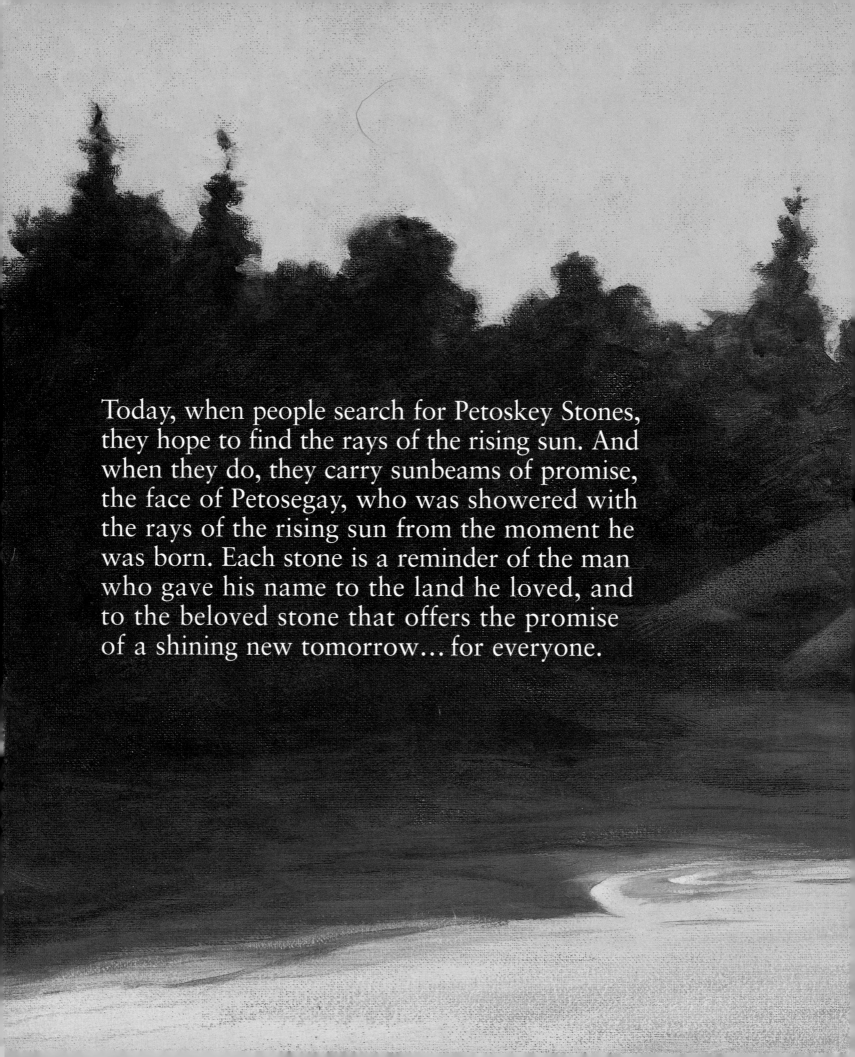

Today, when people search for Petoskey Stones,
they hope to find the rays of the rising sun. And
when they do, they carry sunbeams of promise,
the face of Petosegay, who was showered with
the rays of the rising sun from the moment he
was born. Each stone is a reminder of the man
who gave his name to the land he loved, and
to the beloved stone that offers the promise
of a shining new tomorrow… for everyone.

How to Polish a Petoskey Stone

Adult Supervision Required

After finding your Petoskey Stone, dampen it with water and sand in a rotating fashion with 220 grit sandpaper. When you are finished, rinse and dry your stone. Examine it carefully. If you notice any scratch marks, dampen the stone and sand again. Rinse, dry, inspect, then sand until you are satisfied.

Repeat the process with 400 grit sandpaper to remove coarse spots. Rinse, dry, and examine again.

Now continue the process with 600 grit sandpaper. This will smooth your stone. Rinse, dry, and examine. Repeat with 600 grit sandpaper until your stone is as smooth as it can be.

When you are satisfied, take a piece of dampened corduroy or velvet and sprinkle it with polishing powder. Rub in a small, rotating fashion. If you notice any scratches, go back to the 400 grit sandpaper and repeat the steps from that point on.

When you are finished, rinse and dry your stone. You now have a hand-polished treasure to keep forever!